BUBBLE

By Bryony Storm Dudley

PURPLE UNICORN MEDIA

Published by Purple Unicorn Media

ISBN 978-1-910718-27-8

BUBBLEWOOD

Bryony Storm Dudley

Chapter One

Hello...

They say she feasts on children, they say she's ruthless and cruel. They say she's the face of vengeance itself. But is this true? Or could it be a simple misunderstanding and could she just be nothing but a lonely old lady seeking friendship and love? It's said that she has been seen banqueting over young souls, taking pleasure in enduring the youthful screams of the luckless cherubs. But is this accurate? Or could there be a more bizarre explanation?

My name is Vesta-Ora Marshfield. I live in 2b Bubble-wood House. I moved from the other side of the wood, number one. We had to move because our old house had to be flattened for some reason. I think it was because the man who owns Bubblewood wanted to build a mill or something like that. Mum did tell me but I can't quite remember. Anyway, I live with my mum, dad and my two older siblings, Oscar and Kristie. We also have a dog called Prince. He is the cutest most handsome creature. He has these little adorable perky ears and a coat as soft as winter's snow. We have another addition to the family, this one not so fluffy. My mum adopted my best friend Eve a year ago, after her parents died. It's so sad what happened to them. You see, her mum was a zoo keeper in the local zoo, and that day her dad had to do some volunteering for his CV. So, Eve's mum said that he could do it there. Anyway, so there was this massive black panther and it basically went mad in the section of the zoo and this resulted in it killing her mum and it pushed her dad into a pond and he drowned. Eve still cries about it at night even now. I try to comfort her, but I think she just needs time.

I'm just so lucky to have my mum and dad fit and healthy. My dad works as a builder, which is quite a dangerous job, but he has been building for all his life, so I don't worry about him that much. My mum works in the summer as an event manager, which is cool because me and my friends often get into events for free.

"Guys, dinner." shouted Mum.
We all galloped down the stairs like a herd of ravenous elephants. Once we parked ourselves at the table, Kristie declared that she had an announcement to make.
"Right everyone, I have something to tell you. One of my friends, Bella, said that there was an old woman walking around the house yesterday. Going by the name of 'The S Flower...'"
"For the last time Kristie there is not a witch living in the cottage," Mum claimed as she cut her off.
So, let me get you up to speed. There's a story about a witch who lives in the cottage, number 2a. It's said that she eats children and hunts down any living thing that dares to turn their head her way for just a split second. We all tease her for believing the stories. Although very few people are as gullible as to believe these tales, people do believe that there is a witch living there. And me, well I just think that a little old lady lives in a little cottage in the middle of the woods. People just assume, because it does sound like a very typical scenario.

Chapter Two

Sally Daisy...

"Hey Eve, did you hear about that man who tried to work out the combination for our bridge? It's the two year anniversary today." I stated.
"Oh do you mean the man who got pushed off the bridge by the police before I moved in?" she answered.
"Yeah I think that's the man, although the police didn't mean to push him. Remember there was a big debate about it?"
"Ah yeah, I remember." she said.
"I don't think he deserved to die for trying to break in though, do you?"
"Uh yeah of course, he nearly broke in to our home, didn't it scare you?" she enquired.
"Well yeah but we didn't even live here then. I don't think he deserved that though."

"Vesta, Eve? Do you know what building you're going to do your geography project on? You need to think about it?" quizzed Mum.
She was right, for geography we had to think of a building to do research about. Most of our class were doing it on the school or their house, but me and Eve wanted to do something different.
"No Mum, we're doing it together. We'll think about it tonight." I said.

"Eve, I just had an amazing idea about our project - we can do it on the cottage. That way we'll have to talk to the owner." I said.
"Oh, I don't know Vest, that sounds pretty scary, what if she doesn't like us?"

“Well she will like us. We can do it okay?”
“Well we'd better make sure we have life insurance.” she said so seriously.
“Ha, we don’t need that yet.” I said as I giggled my way down to Mum.
“Mum we had the best idea for our geography project. We're doing it on the cottage.” I said.
“Uh, well I guess you could if you're careful.” she replied, “But don’t be too long, and ring me once you’re finished.”
Honestly, my mother. It's as if she believes that a witch lives in the cottage.

The next day we woke up to Prince barking at a stranger by the front gate. She looked so lost and rather old, we joked about her being the witch.
“Uh who are you and what are you doing upsetting our dog?” I said.
“Oh, sorry girls, my name is Sally Daisy. I work at the school in the reception. Are you Eve and Vesta-Ora Marshfield?” she said.
“Uh yeah that's us, what do you want?”
“Oh, nothing. Don't worry yourselves, goodbye now.”
With that she darted off.
“Well that was weird.” Eve said.
“No, no that was more than weird, I've never heard of a Miss Daisy before.”
“Yeah, you're right. Wait, did she say her name was Sally?”
“Uh yeah I think, why?”
“Well you know they call the witch The S Flower? Do you think that's her... the witch?” Eve said rather dramatically.

Chapter Three

The folder...

"Girls, breakfast time." roared Mum.
We both went to eat but as soon as we got down there, Mum told us that she had a visitor from the school. She said her name was Sally... Sally Daisy.
"Well girls, what do you say to your teacher?" said Mum.
"She's not our teacher mum, we don't even know her." Eve said quite angrily.
"Girls just say hello and don't be so rude."
"Uh hello Miss Daisy." I said, acting like I knew who she was. So that was that - we had to have breakfast with the so-called witch of the wood.

Throughout our little meal she kept on asking Mum questions about me, Oscar, Kristie and Eve, and the worst part was Mum was quite happy answering all of them. None of these questions had anything to do with school, they were questions like "How old were you when you started eating?" and "Can you remember the last time you tidied your rooms?" Mum just thought she was showing an interest in us.

After what seemed like forever, she finally left. We didn't want to bother Mum or annoy her with this whole witch thing, so we just kept it to ourselves for now. After all, we still had to figure out if she was the witch. Which she obviously wasn't because I know that witches don't exist. Do they?

"Kristie, can I ask you something please?" I asked. She said yes, so I asked her about the witch. She told me that they call her the S Flower. I guess that makes sense because daisy is a flower. She also said that her friend went exploring and never came back, but I nodded and widened my eyes like I believed her but obviously I didn't. She told me that she has a fact file all about it because she studied the cottage for the same reason I must. One page said...

* The house looks like an old building

* I can see lots of plants in the garden

* I can only see the top two windows

* The gate is small and wooden

* I can't hear a witch

* I can see a fireplace and smell smoke

* Nobody has come out for a day now

* There are glasses of milk by the gate

"So it looks like someone is in there then?" I asked.
"Yep but who?"

Chapter Four

The Milk man...

The next day, me and Eve went to the cottage to do our geography project.
“Come on Vest, you're walking so slowly.” said Eve.
“Well sorry but I'm trying to be extra careful, just in case she comes out.”
“Oh, I'm too scared, I don't know if I can do it. What if she tries to cook us like on the movies!” she whined.
“Oh, stop being such a baby. No one's going to eat us, now come on then, let’s knock on the door.” I said.

So, we were about to knock the door when we heard the milk man shout “Excuse me out of my way, Mr. Cream won't be happy if his milk is late.”
“Wait, so there's not a witch living there, maybe it's a wizard or an old man.” Eve said, with so much relief in her voice she almost seemed happy.
“Look, maybe it's just the witch's son or something. Or maybe the milk man got it wrong.” I said.

So after that encounter with the milk man we went home and told Kristie. She said that someone goes there very early to meet the milk man, but the milk is not under his name. Kristie acted like she knew everything about the cottage and the witch. We didn’t want to correct her because for some reason she’s really defensive over it; I think she actually enjoys he thrill of living next to a so-called witch. But we still wanted to go and explore the cottage - we needed to for our geography homework.

“Oscar, will you please accompany me and Vesta to the cottage because we think there's a nasty man in there,” Eve claimed.
“Uh sorry Eve but I promised Miss Daisy that I'd go on a walk with her. Mind you, I have no idea why she would want to go for a walk on a Sunday with me, especially to the cottage. Maybe another day, sorry.” he said.
“Uh, okay then”. Eve said quite quietly.

“Vesta, I've just spoken to Oscar and he said that Miss Daisy asked him to go on a walk to the cottage with her, maybe she wants to cook him!” shouted Eve.
“No! Stop being stupid. She won't eat him but I guess it won't hurt to have a little look at what they get up to.” I said.
So that was that. We were going to be spying on our so-called teacher.

We didn’t really have anything planned for today, but our friend Megan was coming over for a bit. We played hopscotch a few times before going to Megan's house for a few hours. Me and Eve didn't want to tell Megan about the witch because she is terrible at keeping secrets. Last year, I told her not to tell anyone that I had brought a frog into school for show and tell but she did.

Chapter Five

The spying experience...

So, the next day was Sunday and at 9 o'clock in the morning Oscar was going on a walk with Mrs. Daisy, and we were spying.
"Wait Oscar, can me and Eve please come with you to do our geography project?" I asked.
"No dear" Miss Daisy said before he had a chance to respond, "It's just me and Oscar today. Can't you do your project another day?"
"Yeah, I guess, but why can't we come with you?"
"Well dear, I would prefer if it were just two of us. You see, I have quite a bad headache."
"Well okay if you're sure." I said in disbelief.
So after about half an hour of us following them they went to the cottage and Miss Daisy started to dust the bugs off the gate.
"Whoa Miss I don't think that you should be touching someone else's property." said Oscar.
"Oh, okay, well where else do you want to go dear?" she asked.
"Uh well I have a question, uh who lives in that cottage? You seem to be very interested in it." he said.
"Uh well a Mr. Cream lives there dear."
"Well, have you ever met him?"
"Uh what's with all the questions dear?" she asked.
"I'm just curious that's all."
"Well you know what they say don't you? Curiosity killed the cat." she said with an evil look in her eyes.

"Well that was weird, she seemed to be hiding something." Eve said.
I agreed with her and we went back home before they did.

We agreed that the next day we would ask our teacher if there was a Miss Daisy who works in the school.

Chapter Six

The records...

"Are you ready for school guys? We are going to be so late. Come on!" screeched Mum.
"We're nearly ready! But mum can we walk to school today please?" Eve asked.
I think she wanted to walk because if mum took us then she would see us going in to the staffroom instead of reception.

We were about to do the password to open the gate, when we noticed a camera.
"What's this doing there? Is it yours?" Eve asked.
"No Eve, why would I put a camera on the gate? Do you think it's recording?"
"Maybe, oh wait, what if someone's trying to figure out the password? Eve said with so much anger in her voice.
"What, you think someone's watching us? What do we do?" I said.
"Well..."
"Oh what do you girls think you're doing recording people's gates?" shouted a rather scary voice.
"Oh no wait officer, this wasn't us, we live in 2b. This was someone else perhaps trying to get our password." I said to the huge officer.
"Did you see who it was?" he said.
"No I'm afraid not officer, but maybe the camera could have fingerprints." I said.
"Well okay child, may I come in and collect it from you?"
"Uh yes, but just in case can I see some ID please?" I said.
He showed us who he was, "Constable Martin." Then turned the camera off, took it with him and said that he will send a letter informing us of what will be done.

“Why did you speak like that?”
“Like what?” I said.
“Like a very posh person.”
“Well he's a policeman, they’re the only people besides your parents and teachers who you have to be nice to.” I said.
“So what are we going to ask Mr. Locket?” said Eve.
“Well we'll just ask if a Sally Daisy works here.” I said.

“Mr. Locket?”
“Yes Eve, what can I do for you?” he said.
“We were just wondering if a Sally Daisy works here?” she said.
“How do you know her?” he said, sounding really panicked.
”Well she came to our house for breakfast the other day. She said she is a receptionist here.”
“What, she came to your house? She doesn't work here. I don't know if I can tell you this girls.” he said.
Mr. Locket has worked in our school for over 30 years.
“Tell us what? Sir you need to tell us”. I said.
“Well okay, Sally Daisy was a student here over 20 years ago.” he said, “She always was a strange child, before she moved up to Comprehensive school. Her primary school teachers told us that she always used to talk to the dolls from when she was in reception all the way up to year 6. When she was 10 she was still talking to things, every child had already grew out of this. Anyway, when she was 11 she started talking to her food. Along with this, she also started to say some weird things. After about a year the school sent her to an asylum for her mental health. Then she ran off. I haven't heard about her since.” he said.
We all were in shock and could hardly speak.
“S-so she has been on the run for over 20 years?” I said.
“That's right girls.” he said.

Chapter Seven

The school folder (Sally Daisy)

We both went through the whole day in school thinking about Sally Daisy and how there must have been more to it than just talking. If it was just talking, surely that couldn't have been enough to send her to a mental asylum. Something must have happened, something big. There must be a catch.

"Mr. Locket, sorry to keep bothering you about Sally Daisy, but we really need to know the full story. She came into our home and started asking random questions about us. She's even started to go on walks with our brother, Oscar." I said.
"Girls, I can't give out personal information like that I'm sorry." he said.
"That's fine Sir, we've got to get back to class." I said.
"Whoa Vest, we need to know, you said it yourself." Eve said.
I told her that I had a plan, how we were going to sneak into the filing room after school, but first we both had to get an after school detention.

"I haven't done my homework because I was too busy sleeping." I told Miss Charm.
"Same." said Eve.
"Well in that case girls you can both come back and do it after school tomorrow."
That was that, I never knew it was that easy to get a detention.

"Quick Eve, this is our chance to get out." I said.
At that point I was so scared of getting caught but at the

same time the adrenalin rush was killing me.
"Mrs. we need the toilet." I said as she allowed us to leave early.
We stumbled over each other trying to get out of the door. Then we darted to the filing room.
"Whoa young ladies, where do you think you're going?" said Mr. Locket.
"Oh Miss Charm let us go early." I said.
He let us past but we bumped into the school caretaker, Mr. Bead. Luckily he failed to see the two tumbling children who shot past him.

Once we finally got to the room it was locked! So we ran to reception and told them that we needed the key to the toilet. My dad once told me how to use a key to open any door, so that's what we did.
"Right. Now we're finally in here, let's look for Sally Daisy." I said.

"Hang on," Eve said, "Who is Alex Cream?"
"Well the only Cream I know is Mr. Cream from the cottage. You don't think it could be him do you?" I said.
"Well have a look." Eve said impatiently.
Once we opened the file we saw the name Sally Daisy and immediately knew that it had something to do with the cottage but we just had to figure out what.

Chapter Eight

Alex Cream...

This was what the folder looked like...

* Alex was a student here many years ago

* Alex was a teacher here when he was 20

* When Sally Daisy was 11 years old she started to tell Alex about the talking food.

* He believed Sally about the talking food and after we sent her to the asylum Alex pleaded with us but we just thought he was crazy as well so we sent him off too.

* Unfortunately they ended up going to the same asylum.

* When Sally was 22 and Alex was 40, they both ran off and we have no idea of their whereabouts.

* Some also say that they both live in no. 2a bubble-wood cottage

* Also Sally is said to be the creator of some food that can talk. Also Alex Cream goes to the cottage every morning to collect the milk and paper. Obviously that is absurd.

"Whoa, well that was unexpected." I said.

"Come on, let's get back without anyone knowing." Eve said.

We went to give the keys back and then ran to the bridge. Once we got home, me and Eve decided that we were going to spy on the cottage at midnight.

"Right, so at midnight we're going to sneak out and hide behind some trees until they go in?" Eve asked.

"Yes for the 100th time, Eve." I said.

Chapter Nine

Midnight crisis...

So now it is 3 hours until we are due to go spying again. We were sitting in the attic looking over the back gate, trying to figure out how we were going to sneak out at midnight. Then at midnight we crept down the stairs and unlocked the back door.
"Quick, come on Eve." I screeched as she argued back. We finally got down to the tree that we were going to stay behind. Meanwhile, Sally had a camera in her house which showed the front door. She also had put together a circuit which turns the lights on and off. Unfortunately the circuit broke so Sally called Alex to go down to the cottage with him to help fix it. We heard a noise like two voices, a man's and a woman's. So we stood back a little but we both fell into a deep dark hole.

"Ugh, are you okay Eve?" I whispered ever so quietly as we didn't know where we were.
"Yeah, was you knocked out?" Eve said.
"I think, I don't know, anyway do you know where we are?" I said.
"I think we must have fallen down a hole, maybe a well or something." Eve said.

We both were scraping frantically, trying to climb back up, but it was no use. After a while we both fell asleep and awoke to loud voices. One of them sounded like Sally's. The other, well it sounded like an old man. Then Sally's voice got closer and closer. She was climbing down a ladder, but how we didn't see the ladder I don't know.

We saw a massive box of giant straws and hid behind them.
"While I check the electric box, you go and check on the food." Sally said.
Sally was down here with us - what if she smelt a rat, heard us? We had nowhere to go.

Sally had a really tall hook in her hand. She used it to push the very high door open.
"How does she know how to open the door?" Eve asked, sounding shocked and scared.
"Maybe she lives here." I said under my breath.
"What do you mean she lives here? She can't live here, Mr. Cream does!" said Eve.
"Well maybe they're married."

"I know what we should do, we should knock on the door tomorrow to do our geography homework." I said.
"Yeah okay, but first we need to figure out how to get out of here, we can't stay the night." Eve pointed out.

So we tried so hard to get out of there, but it was no use. Then we saw that there was a ladder, so we tried to reach it, but we just couldn't. We realised that Sally had left her big hook so we grabbed it, pulled the ladder down and ran home.

"Well that was a very strange day." I said.
"You can say that again." Eve said.

Chapter Ten

Geography homework...

So in an hour we were going to go to the cottage to do our geography homework.
"What if she's not there?" Eve asked.
"Well I've planned out that at 11 o'clock in the night, she will be there but any earlier she won't." I said.
"What? Won't she think it's a bit weird that we are doing our homework so late?" Eve pointed out.
"Well we'll just say that we forgot and it's our last day to get it done."

We stumbled across the woods until we were just feet away from the surprisingly noisy cottage.
"Oh I don't know anymore Vest, what if she is a witch and she puts us in her cauldron!"
"Don't be so silly Eve, she's not."
"Well, that makes me feel a lot better." said Eve sarcastically.

"Right come on Eve, you can say it and I'll knock." I said.
"Wait, I'm knocking you can say it." she said.
"Say what then?"
"Well say, 'Hello my name is Vesta and this is Eve, we have decided to do our geography homework on your cottage. Could we please ask you some questions?'" Eve said.
"Well that would have been okay if Sally didn't know us." I pointed out.
"Well, won't she have some explaining to do as well?" Eve said, sounding very pleased with herself.

“Okay, I'll start saying it and then when we see Sally we'll act really shocked and surprised okay?” I said. Eve agreed but also pointed out that Mr. Cream might answer the door so I said that I would just say the whole thing.

We walked up to the old tree-like door and Eve knocked it so hard.
“Who is it?” shouted a voice that sounded like Sally's.
“Uh hello could we talk to you for a second please?” I said.
“Uh go away.” she said trying to sound like an old woman.
“Open up Miss Daisy we know you’re in there!” I shouted.
“Wow Vest, what are you doing?” Eve whispered.
“Shoosh.” I said.
“Sorry girls, but I don't know a Sally Daisy.” she said.
“We didn't say Sally, we only said Miss Daisy so quit acting stupid and open up!” I shouted.

She came out wearing normal clothes, nothing that looked like something a witch would wear.
”What are you doing in Mr. Cream's cottage?” Eve said, “Have you cooked him?”
“Eve, she's not a witch, are you?” I said.
“No of course I'm not. Anyway what are you doing here so late?” asked Sally.
“Wow we asked you first so come on why are you here?” I said, looking at Eve; she was looking quite scared.
“Well I'm a cleaner for Mr. Cream.” she said.
“Oh come off it, we know you're not his cleaner. So real reason now or I'm calling the police.” I said.
“Oh Okay, follow me.” She said.

She took us into the cottage, AND...

I was told to sit down and then they explained it all to me. They said that mum was in school with Sally Daisy, and that mum thought Sally was crazy too. Mum's the one who told the school that she was talking to the food, they said. I couldn't believe that mum started the whole thing, Mum seems so innocent.

"So tell me why she told you and not me, Oscar." I yelled.
"Alright, calm down, she thought that you might tell people, you were only 3 when she told me." he said rather smugly.
"OH I hate you!" I spat in disgust, running out of the cottage and vowing never to return.

"Wow, what did I do?" asked Oscar, sounding very worried.
"Oh she's just annoyed that mum didn't tell her, and she told you. Does Kristie know too?" snarled Eve.
"No, she's already superstitious about the cottage, she'll tell everyone." whispered Oscar, in fear of someone hearing and telling Kristie.
"She could have just told her when she was older!" Eve shouted, running after me.

"Mum how could you not tell me? You knew how I felt about it." I snapped.
"What on earth are you talking about Vest?" she asked, acting like she had no idea of the mess she has made.
"Uh about you tidying her room." Eve said, trying to cover the truth.
She pulled me out of the room and said that we could get revenge on mum.
"What kind of revenge?" I asked intrigued. She said that we had to go somewhere else to discuss this.

Chapter Twelve

The Great Plan...

We got Oscar and went to a den that me and Eve made in the woods years ago.
"Why are we here?" Oscar asked, trying to make us let him go home.
"First of all we need to know we can trust you not to say anything to mum." I said.,"About Sally."
"No, sorry girls but I'm not getting involved. Dark things might happen if you mess with stuff like this." he said, "Promise me that you'll leave it alone?"
"What no way." I said, but I was soon to change my mind when I received a deadly, icy glare from Oscar.
"Okay." I said in a very high-pitched voice.

"Wow, I never knew Oscar could be that scary." said Eve.
"Well Oscar is never usually that scary, but when it comes to secrets, especially ones that could harm people, he is very serious." I said.
I looked out the window only to see Oscar storming down the path towards our house.

"Will he stay angry at us Vest?" Eve said.
"I don't think he is mad at us, he probably just needs five minutes." I said reassuringly, "Listen Eve, we are still going to come up with a plan to see the little foods without mum knowing." I said with a panicky tone.
"What, no you can't, Oscar said not to and besides, they will be gone soon." Eve said trembling.
"Yes that is exactly my point." I said, "We need to come up with a way to see them after they go."
"And how are you planning to do that?" she said.

"Well, meet me back at home in half an hour, I need to check something." I said running off.

I ran to the cottage, snuck round the back and acting like a ninja, I went into the room where all of the food was and examined them. Yes that probably does sound really odd, but there is a perfectly reasonable explanation.

So basically the food are very interesting and clever. So I sat down, looked at the food and started to take notes. Then I heard Sally coming so I ran back out the back door and went home to meet Eve.

"So come on then, what's your great plan?" Eve asked.
"Well, you know the food?" I said.
"Yeah, wait the real ones?" asked Eve.
"Yeah anyway I think that we might be able to teach them how to speak so that they can say things to mum." I said rather intelligently.
"Well that is quite a good idea, but won't Sally notice them talking?" Eve said.
"Well yeah but she won't mind."

Okay, after we both agreed that that was a good idea, we tried to think when Sally would be out so we could start. The next day Sally came to the door and asked Mum if we could baby-sit Sally's daughter.
"Uh yeah, I don't see why not, they aren't busy." said mum.
"Marvellous, well come on then girls it's only for a few hours." Sally said.
At this point we were very confused because Sally doesn't have a daughter.

So we walked out into the boiling hot sun with Sally.

“Uh Sally do you really have a daughter?” I asked because we weren't sure she did.

“Yeah, Tori, but I just need you to baby-sit the food for a few hours because I need to go into town to get some saucepans and pots to cook the food in.” she said.

“Wait - the food? You cook them?” Eve said in utter shock.

“Well yes I do but they like it, it’s like a jacuzzi for them.”

“But what happens after that? Do you eat them?” I asked.

"Well I don’t, but once they are ready to go then they slide down the throat and then they are in a new world. Well it’s not a world to us, it’s a place about an hour away from here called Big Mouth. It’s literally a big mouth that stands proudly against a cliff. Although it isn’t real, it sure does look it. The purpose of this is to show the food what it would be like to be eaten because they all want to, but the sad truth about being eaten is that you can’t come back from that. This mouth is a sort of simulator. The foods think that they are being eaten so this way they can have what they want without being harmed. They get swallowed and end up in the stomach, which is huge to the food so they stay there for years, until they want to climb back up the throat to come back.” Sally said.

“Oh well that sounds like something out of a book, like fiction or a fairy tale.” I said ever so sarcastically.

“Oh no dear, this is not fiction, this is one hundred percent real. Listen, if you want to then once Coco is ready then you can watch him enter the mouth.” Sally said.

“Well is Big Mouth easy to find?” I asked.

“Well, only if you have a secret pass.” she explained.

So now I understood, and she told me that Coco was the eldest food there. In a few weeks I was going to watch Coco get eaten!

“Right then, Eve and Vesta. Are you ready for your presentation?” my geography teacher asked as my hands trembled.
I wasn’t scared to talk in front of the class, just afraid if we give away too much detail about the cottage. We were going to do the school instead after we found out about the food but we had already told our teacher that we chose the cottage.

We walked up to the front of the class with 20 pairs of eyes staring back at us. Once we had finally finished speaking miss said the worst thing that she possibly could have said,
“Any questions?”
Oh no, what were we going to do?

“Who lives in there?” asked Martha.
Oh that silly girl, I had to pass this one on to Eve.
“Eve would you like to tell them?” I asked as I could feel her eyes staring sharply at me.
“Yeah well um an old woman, she is very lovely.” Eve said as it was quite obvious that she had just been put on the spot.

After the speech we all went home. I was terrified to tell mum because she was already angry at me that we were going to do our geography project on the cottage but as we all knew, it was too late by then.

We both went to bed with so much excitement about Coco leaving.

Chapter Thirteen

Big Mouth...

The next morning there was a knock on the door, it was Sally and we had forgotten that today we were going to Big Mouth.
"Who is it, Vesta?" asked Mum.
"Uh its Sally, she's taking me and Eve on a shopping trip if that's okay with you Mum." I said.
Mum said that it was fine and we put our shoes on, zipped up our coats and walked to Sally's house.

So once we got there, Sally went in to get Coco, but little did we know that my friend Megan was walking towards us.
"Sally!" we shouted as Megan came closer.
"Vesta, Eve, your mum said that you was here, what are you doing?" Megan shouted.
"Uh hi Megan we were just going on a shopping trip with Sally." I said, trying my best to make her go away.
"Oh that's nice. Where are you going? Can I come?" she said, so fast I could hardly understand what she was saying.
"No sorry dear, there won't be any room in the car." explained Sally.
After nearly twenty minutes of persuading Megan to go, she finally ran off. Sally put Coco in the cold bag and we drove off.

"We have been driving for ages! Are we almost there?" whined Eve trying not to go back to sleep.
"Well girls we are almost at the first gate." said Sally, driving up to the biggest gate you could ever imagine.
"Wow." we both said staring up.
We drove about 2 miles before we came to another gate.

Sally got out of the car and put some kind of pass up against something on the wall. The gate opened slowly and we drove peacefully through.

We drove up and up until we came to a massive cliff. There was a huge man there, so big that you could only see his head unless you looked over the edge. We all got out, Coco was so excited, he was running around and shouting things like "I can't wait to finally meet my dad." After about 10 near panic attacks he finally plucked up the courage to walk up to the mouth. He stepped up onto the tongue and started jumping, but he was quick to stop when Sally told him off.

"Goodbye, I might see you again some time Sally." said Coco trying not to cry.
His mood changed all of a sudden when he sat down getting ready to slide down the throat, he was so excited. He waved vigorously as he slid down.

"Hello, can you help me please?" said a little tube of icing.
Sally went pale. "Hello little one, aren't you a little bit too young to be here?" I said in pure confusion.
"Yeah I am but I'm not here to go down. I have something to tell you. So, basically a few months ago someone put me and my dad on a cake stall in a market. We just ran away." she said.
"Oh my goodness, that is awful, where is your dad now?" I asked.
"I don't know; he was behind me just now but he said he is going for a walk, he will be here soon." she said.
"Right we need to go right now." Sally said.
"What? Why?" I asked.
She just stood there as white as snow.
"Oh I have a question." said Icing. "Could you please adopt me?"

“No sorry dear.” said Sally with obvious fear in her eyes.
“What, why not? You take in food from all over the world, why can't you take Icing in?” Eve asked.
“Fine.” she said, quite clearly hating the idea for some reason.
Suddenly the unimaginable happened...

Chapter Fourteen

WHAT!

“You! No, not you, come away now everyone.” said an old biscuit.
"Is this your dad?” I asked.
"Yeah. Dad, is everything okay?” she asked her dad.
“No dear, everyone step away from Sally Daisy now!” he shouted.
"Why? Look what's going on?” I said slowly walking away from Sally.
“This is the evil creature who put me up for sale!” he shouted at Sally.

Sally went so pale she was almost see-through. She started to run off shouting
“You're worthless”.
We all caught her and made her drive us all back to the cottage. The drive back was fairly quiet, well apart from the odd question to Sally but she was driving in silence.

Once we got back we decided not to ask Sally any questions because we didn’t want to hear her excuses. We told her that she had two options. One being that she left the cottage for good, or two that we make up a lie to tell the police. So she chose to leave the cottage.

The next day it was raining cats and dogs; Sally wasn't very happy. She packed her bags, said goodbye to the foods and drove off in a state. We could hear her shouting things at us.

Things had become a lot quieter over the past few weeks. We kept popping in to see the five foods who were,

Icing, Bissy, Milky, Jammy and the super girly girl Zaza. Icing was a lovely tube of pink icing, Bissy was the oldest biscuit ever. Milky was a very delicate and wise bottle of milk, Jammy was a super sweet jar of strawberry jam and Zaza was a long pizza baguette.

We spent every weekend having sports days, but mum could never know, her dark past was behind her we could never bring it back. We also taught them how to speak properly. We were like a little family, well for the moment at least.

Chapter Fifteen

The visitors...

So it was just after we finished our game of football, there was a tremendously loud knock on the door.
"Who could that be?" I said in panic, "Quick, hide the food, I'll answer the door."
I walked up to the short brown door, my legs wobbling like jelly. I opened the door and a familiar face glared at us.
"Hello, it's me Tori, sorry can me and Ashleigh come in please?" said Tori, sounding like she needed to get something off her chest.
"Uh yeah sure, who's Ashleigh?" I asked.
"Oh Ashleigh is my beautiful shiny black cat." she said with pride.

They came in and explained that once Sally had come home to Tori's house, where Tori, Sally and Tori's grandad Paul lived. She said that her grandad was looking for a house and that he didn't want Tori to be around Sally. So that's why Tori was here.

So we made up a room upstairs for Tori and her cat Ashleigh to sleep. Nothing really happened for a few weeks, but then something happened. We were just playing tag in front of the cottage when Megan showed up.
"Hello Eve, hello Vesta. Uh who are you?" she said pointing to Tori.
"Umm hello, I'm Tori I'm their friend." Tori said rather uncomfortably.
"Anyway, what are you doing here again?" Eve asked.
"Well your mum said that I would find you here, do you live here Tori?"
"Uh yeah I just moved in with my mum." she said.

After about an hour of trying to convince Megan to leave, she finally fled.

We continued to play when suddenly Tori screamed as she fell down the well.
"Don't worry, we'll open the cellar door you can get through that way!" we shouted down to her.
Meanwhile, little did we know that Tori had company down the well.

We ran down to the cellar as fast as we could. We turned the door handle, and ran down to Tori to see if she was alright. She was just sitting there staring at an old woman.
"Who are you?" I asked in fright, "What are you doing in our cellar?"
"Hello girls sorry to bother you, is there a woman by the name of Sally Daisy living here?" she asked in a croaky voice.
"Uh who's asking?" Eve asked quite reasonably.
"Uh I live here, well I used to at least."
"What do you mean you live here? No one lives here, my mum Sally used to but no one does now." Tori said sounding quite defensive.
"You are Sally's daughter? Look I'm sorry but you might have heard of me before." the old lady said.
"Why? The only other person who is said to of lived here is the witch." I said.
"Well there you go then..."

Chapter Sixteen

Beth...

"What? No, you can't be. Prove it!" I shouted.
"Calm down, look everyone, I know all about the foods. I know everything, I even have my own loaf of bread. This is Esty." the old woman said pulling out a loaf of beautiful golden bread.
"Wow." we all said in synchrony.
"What's your name then? How old are you? Where do you come from?" Eve said making no sense.
"Wow easy on the interrogation, my name is Beth and I am a supreme witch. I'm originally from Canada but when I was about 10 me and my family moved to Japan for my father's work. Then a bomb hit the part of Japan we were living in and it killed all of my family. My brother, mum and dad. I was 20 at the time. I flew over here to England and got married but then I divorced about 25 years ago. Then I got into witchcraft and now I'm here."

We were all so amazed by her story that we told her to come upstairs and sit down. We took Esty into the room with the other foods to meet them. They were a bit jumpy at first but after a few hours they got to know her and really liked her. We sat down at the table in the living room and talked for what seemed like for ever, although it was probably just two hours which is still a pretty long time. She was just telling us all about how her witch-crafting came about.

After we had talked for so long we decided to check on Esty. She was telling the other foods all about her journey here.
"Wow that sounds like a lot of fun, how old are you?"

asked Jammy.
“I'm 7, but I don’t go to Big Mouth because when I was two years old my mum forgot to take me and nothing happened to me so I'm here now.” Esty said with pride.
“Wow, you’re so lucky, I wish I could stay here. Wait isn't that the same thing that happened to you dad?” asked Icing.
"Yeah dear, it is and I'm not going to lie and say it was easy because it wasn't. I had to work for my mother everyday.” he said.

“Do you want to stay here with us for a little while?” I asked Beth.
“Uh yeah okay if it’s not too much of a hassle, I would love to sleep in my house again.” she said.
So we spent most of the day making her room up, but there was a few hours left to go shopping.
“Right then off we go, I do love a good clothes shop. Oh and I've seen some beautiful tops in that shop by the train station." Eve said.
“Really? The one with those models in the window?” I said.
“Okay I have no idea where that is or what you're talking about, but it sounds like fun, you can never have enough clothes.” Tori said.

We were walking across the old bridge, which I certainly think should be sorted out, the number of pot holes is unreal. Anyway we made our way half way across it doing cartwheels, when suddenly we came to a rather unexpected stop. The thing is that where we live is a wood and the only way to enter is across the bridge. There is a ten digit combination to open the super tall gate and only the two families which is mine and the cottage knows it. So if someone else wants to get in like the postman then he will ring the phone which my mother will answer and open the gate from the house. Anyway this must mean that mum let them in! She let the police in, and my teacher?

"Hello young ladies, have you got a moment?" my teacher said.
"Mr. Clove? Uh hello, how did you get in here?" I asked.
"Oh well, your mum let me in, although I needn't bother her. I've come to ask you some questions." he said.
"Well we won't keep you sir, we were just about to go down to town so if you don't mind." I said walking away and directing him to the gate.
"Beth. Ring any bells?" he said smugly. We froze and slowly turned around.
"Beth?" I said. "No never heard of her."
"Let me introduce you to P.C Lowri. Maybe she could tell you how serious this is." he said.
I mean I knew he wasn't the nicest teacher but this, this is a whole new level. I decided that this was enough so I shouted at my teacher! Could I get in trouble for that? It was outside of school. I would be fine right? Here I go.
"Right okay sir, sorry to have to do this but get out of this wood. You are a horrible man; you are terrorising young children!"
"Tori, look scared." I whispered.
"Get out of our homeland, Now!" There you go, I shouted at my teacher; phew.
"How dare you speak to me like that, you shall have detention for ever!" he shouted as he crossly stormed out of the gate with the police woman tailing after him.

"Right, let's quickly run back, we need to tell Beth that the police were looking for her." I said.
So we darted back to the ridged cottage and shouted.
"Beth!"
"What is it? Is everyone okay?" she replied.
"We don't know what you have done but there was a

police woman looking for you with our teacher." I said rather crossly.
"Lowri, I knew that wretched girl wouldn't keep away." she squealed.
"What do you mean? Do you actually know her?" Tori asked her seeming rather surprised.
"Sit down girls I have something I think you ought to know." she said pleading with us to come closer as if we were a pack of dogs.

"So it all started back about 30 years ago when I was just starting witchcraft. I needed to practice because believe it or not I wasn't very good at it, anyway in my old house we had quite a big attic so I would spend all my spare time doing spells up there." she said pointing to the roof.
"Wait - you used to live here all those years ago?" I asked.
"Yes I did indeed, it was a very pleasant place. So as I was saying, I always did my spells in the attic but one day out of the bluc there was a loud knock on the front door. I lived with my friends at that time but they were all far too lazy to answer the door so it was left to me. 'Hello?' I said as I slowly opened the door. Standing there was a police woman, she said that she had come to investigate some smoke from the house. I knew immediately that someone had seen the smoke from my spells. She said that the woman at number one had spotted smoke. An old woman called Dorothy lived there for a few years." she said.

We talked for a while and she told us how P.C Lowri went up to the attic and found a lot of smoke.
"I needed to confess but not of the right crime. I told her that I was trying to set the house on fire." she said,
"The only one of my friends who believed me was Sally Daisy." she said really quietly.
"Sally Daisy? You knew Sally all those years ago?" I

shouted.
“Yes we lived together but I wasn't really her friend. We knew each other through our friend Connor.” she said, “I never liked her much at all.” she moaned, you could tell that her past had come flooding back to her memory.

After our long talk, Beth asked us if we wanted to go up to the old crusty attic to see if her cauldron was still there. So we all nervously crept past the foods’ room, up the fragile stairs and pushed open the wonky door. We were in.
“Let me have a little look.” she said as she rummaged through the attic, “Ah I found it, this was last used over 30 years ago.” she said blowing cob webs off of a huge black bowl looking thing.
“Is that the cauldron? Is that thing dangerous?” Tori asked.
"This is the almighty cauldron, the one that I used to make my Friday night pizza baguette into Zaza.” she said as if she was proposing a speech.
“Wait - you made Zaza in here? Did you make everyone else too?” Eve asked.
“Yes I did and I'm very proud of all of them.” she announced.

Beth took the cauldron down to the living room and washed it out.
“Wait - how did Sally know about the food if you were here first?" Eve said sounding as if she was trying to defend Sally.
“Well, girls,” she said as she was clearly about to start telling a story, “You see after I got dragged out of the cottage, Sally whispered into my ear and asked me if I wanted her to look after the cauldron. I said no, I shouted no, but she didn't listen. When they finally let me go, I came home to find that the house was empty. No one was there, no one’s stuff was there, and my beloved

cauldron…" she whined.
"So my mum stole your cauldron?" Tori asked in disbelief.
"Yeah she did, she was not a very nice person but I didn't think she could be that horrid." Beth snapped.

We decided to stop upsetting Beth and told her to lay low for a few days just in case of any surprise visits from P.C Lowri. We waited for a few hours before we decided to try going shopping again. We had a brilliant day out shopping, we bought quite a lot of clothes. We skipped back across the bridge debating whether we should go back to the cottage to check on Beth. In the end we decided that we were going to pop in and see her. We slowly walked up to the door and knocked. No one answered so we peeked through the window and we saw Beth holding something. It looked like a pass, to Big Mouth!

Chapter Seventeen

The pass...

We all glared at each other and ran to my house in utter shock.
"Did she have a pass to Big Mouth?" I asked trying to catch my breath.
There was quite a long pause.
"Yes I think, but how did she get it?" Eve asked.
Then my phone rang... I looked at it as if it was a disgusting vile creature.
"Well, who is it?" Tori asked.
I dropped my phone on the cold ground.
"It's Sally..." I whispered.
"Sally? What could she possibly want?" Eve said in utter disgust.
"Well are you going to answer it?" Tori asked as it she wanted to speak to her.
"No of course I'm not!" I said.
"But maybe she has some news or something. I've blocked her number so maybe she wants to speak to me." Tori said desperately.
So after about 20 minutes of us debating whether to call her back or not, we had missed over 10 calls from her.
"Right that's enough. Let's just ring her back yeah?" I said.
They both agreed that if she kept calling back then she needed something urgently.
"Okay here we go." I said in fear of hearing her voice once again.

"Hello listen girls, I know we aren't exactly best friends but I need your help. " she cried.

“What is it then? Another fake plan? ” I said.
“No I need to tell you something listen, it’s Beth, she's got my pass to Big Mouth.”
This all sounded very dramatic but in all reality, the shock just wasn’t there. It was probably because we were used to getting surprised.

“What do you want us to do about it?” I asked Sally.
“Well girls I need you to get it back for me.”
“Wait - you don’t have any food to take there so why do you need it?” I argued.
“Well I am still adopting foods you see I have a little egg called Elgar, she needs to go to Big mouth.”
“No, we need to get her off you. You might sell her or something. Please Sally, do us one final favour and save Elgar.” I said rather dramatically.
“I'm not going to do anything to Elgar, look all I want is for you to hand me the pass so I can take her to Big Mouth.” she said.
We thought for a while but we knew that she couldn’t be trusted.

“Sorry Sally but we aren't going to give you the pass, look I know that you can be rather horrid when it comes to the food so it’s a no.” I said whilst hanging up.
We all giggled for a minute but we were soon to stop when we heard a voice from my phone,
“Hello? Girls I'm still here, please give me the pass, think about poor Elgar.” she said.
“Well if you're that worried about her then we'll take her to Big Mouth for you. That way she won't be in any danger.” Tori said.
“Tori? Is that you? Please, my beautiful daughter, help mummy.” she said desperately.
“That’s flattering mum, it really is but you betrayed me so

I'm sorry mum but Beth is looking after me now so I don't need you and nor does Elgar." Tori said a little sarcastically.

We decided to hang up and frankly we were all sick and tired of secrets, well harmless ones anyway. So we went to confront Beth.

"Uh hi Beth, what are you doing?" I asked.

"Oh girls, hello I was just doing some cheese on toast, want some?" she said.

"Umm yeah okay, can we ask you something please?"

"I'm afraid I may already know what you're about to say." she interrupted, "Sit. Listen, it's about Sally. She just rung me. She was on the phone to you right?"

"Yeah about a pass right?" I said.

"Yes, look, many years ago I stole her pass just like she did my cauldron and she thought she lost it so she paid a lot of money for a new one, the last ever one. Once I found out about what she did to the foods, I cut up the pass in front of her. Then she rang me to check up on you Tori, but little did I know that she was on video call and she saw the pass and shouted 'You have the last ever pass!' I froze then she must have rung you." she said in a bit of a state.

We were all as shocked as each other. Beth thought that Sally may return in the night so she advised us to stay over at the cottage. I ran home quickly to tell mum that we were staying over Megan's, while Beth made up three beds for us in the spare room. We were all in the foods' room telling ghost stories until gone midnight. It was scary because every so often one of us would scream in an attempt to horrify the other one.

"And they all lived horribly ever after." I said as I told the ending of my story.

"That was by far the scariest story I've ever heard. I love

stuff like this, you know when we can all get together and terrify each other!" Zaza said with a wicked cry in her cackle.

We went to sleep at about 2 o'clock in the morning. It was quite scary sleeping next to Tori as she kept doing really weird things in her sleep like rubbing her "Blanky" all over the bed. She even fell off the bed twice.
"Wakey wakey, rise and shine, time to get up, it's morning time!" came the loud voice of Beth from deep downstairs.
"Cheese on toast alright?" she shouted up.
We all replied with a simple "Yes please."
Once we had eaten we went to let off some steam by running round the garden almost 6 times. Beth said that running was a way of the wise or something like that. Beth was always giving us meaningful advice and quotes, she's sort of the wise old woman of us all. Anyway, after we'd almost collapsed we decided to play a little bit of Frisbee before going back to mine to ask mum a question that was curdling on our minds.

"OH I nearly caught it, AH! I stood on a stone." shouted Tori.
We were just about to go over to see if she was okay when the side gate swung open.
"Please, I need the pass." Sally screamed as she rather dramatically threw herself through the gate.
"Sally? What on earth are you doing here, Eve, call the police!" I shouted.
"No please wait, I just need to say that I really need my pass, you have no right over it. Please, it's mine. I need to take Elgar; you don't understand she only has 4 weeks." she said.
"Where is Elgar then?" Tori asked.
"She's in my mini portable fridge."
"Your mini portable fridge?" I said in utter disbelief.

But she wasn't lying, she pulled out a very small fridge and opened it. There was the smallest, the cutesiest and the most adorable egg.

"Pass her here, look we need to take her now. You can not be trusted. Sorry Sally, but we need to take her." I said.
"How can I trust you, you're only kids. I'm experienced. I made Big Mouth." she blurted out.
We all glared at her in utter shock.
"You said that you had no idea how Big Mouth came about, why would you lie to us all mum?" Tori asked.
"Because I knew that you would all take advantage of it and try to go there as often as you like and tell people about it, as if it was my workplace." she explained.
"Right, well now we know that you will never tell us anything that's not a lie ever again!" Tori shouted as she darted off into the woods.
I ran after her because she was heading to where they knocked our old house down, it's a huge building site. Tori didn't know her way around the woods she would probably get lost if I didn't chase her.

"Hey Tori, you might not be that bad at a running race. Where are you going?" I asked.
"I just want to be on my own. I can't believe she is the mastermind behind Big Mouth. I'm her only child, how could she keep that from me?" she cried.
"Hey cheer up, you know I almost fell over a branch chasing you, imagine if you looked and you saw me lying on the floor wriggling like a worm." I said while she was giggling; although it wasn't much it was still there.
"What's down here? Eve told me that you and her used to live down there." she said pointing down a rather steep hill.
"Well she got some of that right. You see that big floor of concrete, that's where our house used to be before the

council knocked it down." I explained.
"What? Why did they knock it down? Were you all homeless?" she said in panic.
"No. They had to build a wind farm or something." I said, sounding like I knew what I was on about, but as you can probably imagine I had no idea.
I hoped and prayed that she wouldn't question me. No her mouth was opening!
"What's a wind farm? " she asked.
Ah no! I had no idea myself; I just had to be truthful.
"I have absolutely no idea what so ever." I said as she again quietly giggled.

After a long while of me persuading her to come back we finally did.
"Where is she?" Tori asked.
"Don't worry, I got rid of her ages ago." Eve said.
We got the food together and asked them what they wanted to do, seeing as we hadn't really spent much time with them lately.
"We don't want to do anything, but we do think that you should go to see your mum. You haven't in a while, she might start to get suspicious." Jammy said.
They were right, but we couldn't take them for obvious reasons so we snuck them up to our attic just in case Sally made a very unwanted appearance. Mum always told me, Oscar, Eve and Kristie to never lie to her. This wasn't lying right? This just wasn't telling.

We needed to see Sally for one last time before we went home, to trick her into leaving us alone. She wanted the pass so we were going to give her it, well a fake version. She should be grateful - a fake version is better that none at all right?
"Come on then in you get, welcome to my car." Beth said rather proudly.

I'm pretty sure that witches moved around on broomsticks. Well not this one. So we got in the smelly car and drove off to a park that Sally lives near. We told Tori to wait in the car if she didn't want to see Sally. In the end we all went in to the park. No sign of her. Wait I spoke too soon.
“Sally listen we have the pass for you, in agreement that you leave us alone.” I proposed.
“What this must be some kind of wind up. Why would you give it to me now?” she said.
“Well we have decided to give you what you want for the sake of the food, they are too innocent to be used as a threat.” Tori said.
“Well okay then.” she said, giggling to herself as she ran away.

We got home quite late as we stopped off to get some security things for the cottage so Sally wouldn't be able to get in. Then, Beth, Tori and Eve went inside, while I went to the house to get the food.
“Why are you back so late? I haven't seen you and Eve in so long - not properly.” Mum said.
“Yeah sorry mum, it’s just that Tori is having some trouble with her homework and we're helping her. It’s a very long project but we are almost half way through.” I said, trying my best to improvise.
“Okay, so I will start to see you more then?” she said.
“Mum, you see us all the time anyway.” I snapped, “Sorry, I didn't mean that, I'm going to the cottage I’ll see you tomorrow.”

I felt so bad about shouting at her, I'll make it up to her somehow. I know, I'll spend the whole of tomorrow with her.
“Hi Tori, listen, I'm sorry but me and Eve are going to spend the whole day with Mum tomorrow because she is starting to get very suspicious.” I said.

“That's okay, don’t worry, we were going to have a bit of a spring clean anyway.” Tori said quite happily.
“Alright then, well you don't mind if we go now do you?” I asked.
She told me to stop being so silly and have fun so we went home.

Chapter eighteen

A day with mum...

"Hi mum, we're going to spend the whole day with you tomorrow," I said, "Sorry we haven't been here much."
"Don't be silly girls, come on let's have a movie night and then tomorrow we can go to the park and we'll have ice cream." Mum said.
"Sounds good."

"Go on then Vest, get the popcorn, Eve get the chocolate and strawberries." Mum ordered.
"What film are we going to watch?" Eve asked.
"That one you said you liked." she answered.
About half way through the film, Mum paused it and asked us a question, a question so mind boggling and brain frying that I froze for like 10 seconds, but still it was scary.
"Girls I need to ask you a question. It's about Sally, please tell me she didn't leave because of the food." she said sounding rather concerned.
"The what?" Eve said trying to cover up the fact that we have both been involved with the food for a few months now.
"Don't even try to play innocent Eve, I know everything." she said quite crossly.
Well we thought she was cross but we needed to make sure of it.
"Are you cross at us?" I asked.
"No girls, I'm just disappointed that you didn't tell me."
Well she wasn't cross, she was just disappointed - which was worse?

So we had no choice but to talk. Dad was at work and he didn't get back till about midnight, but did Dad

know?
"Okay then mum we'll tell you everything. Sally told us that she worked at the school and you believed her!" I shouted.
"No girls, I knew from the very start, I have known and hated Sally Daisy for years." Mum said.
We were in utter shock at this point.
"Girls, I need you to tell me what Beth has said and what you have been doing."
"Well we met up with Sally earlier and gave her a fake pass to Big Mouth. She said that she will leave us alone if we gave her one, she didn't say she wanted a real one though." I said.
"Wait, she wanted a pass…?!"

"Uh yeah, but we didn't give her a real one. "
"Do you know why she wanted one? Well I do. The pass that you all share is the only one left in the world, the only Big Mouth pass. Sally made them, she made them so that no one could ever make another one, even Sally. Once she finds out that it's fake she is going to go spare. We have to be very careful." Mum said.
"I still don't understand why she wants the pass." Eve said.
"Eve, why do you think? If she can't have Big Mouth then no one can. She's going to close it all down."
"What? But she can't do that, she can't. Mum you need to change the code on the gate."
"Way ahead of you girls, I changed it last week. I had my suspicions."

So Mum knew everything but now we needed to tell everyone else.
"Hello guys, we have something to tell you." Eve said as Mum walked in.
"What, who's that?" Tori asked in panic.

“This is my mum, Louise.” I said as Tori and Beth stared, “Don't worry, she knows all about the food.”
“What, you told her? Vesta!” Tori shouted.
“Well kind of, she already knew. Her and Sally were at school together, she's known since then.” I said.
“She was told that all of the food died.”
“What? That must have been awful, was it? Please tell us all about it.” Tori said showing such interest.

“Okay well I was at school with Sally back when we were both 11, like you lot. She had always been somewhat strange, but we never knew she could be sent to an insane asylum. Me and Olivier, my best friend at the time were in the dinner queue when Sally started staring at something. It was a carton of milk, she started saying things like ‘It’s okay little fella, I’ll save you.’ We just thought she was crazy and after a few more times of this happening, someone told our history teacher, Mr. Cream. All he did was pretend to see them too, well at least we thought he was pretending. So Olivier told our headteacher, Mr. Bran. He straight away admitted them both to an insane asylum. And the last I've heard is that they both escaped together.” she said.

“Well that was a story, so how did you know that the food was real?” Tori said in disbelief.
“Well I was at home watching TV when there was a knock at the door. My mum told me to answer it so I did and it was Sally. She told me that she wasn't crazy, but I just closed the door on her. But then she posted a little rasher of bacon through the letter box. It had eyes, arms and legs. It had a big grin on its face and it said ‘Hello, my name is Belle.’ It was the cutest thing ever. So I believed her and then we just became friends. One day she told me that she created this place where the food could go after 2 years to

be free, she called it Big Mouth." she said.
"It all makes sense now." Tori said.

Chapter Nineteen

The lost girl...

We decided to go to the park for a bit to burn off some energy. We got there and started to play frisbee when we heard a strange crying noise coming from the trees.
"Shh, what's that noise? It sounds like someone crying." Eve said. We slowly walked towards the weeping girl.
"Hello? What's you're name?" I asked.
"I'm Dollie." she said still in tears.
"What's the matter?"
"I've lost my dog." she cried.
"Oh how?" I asked.
"I don't know, one minute he was here and then the next he just vanished".

"Okay, calm down, don't worry everything is going to be okay. How old are you?" Tori asked making out that everything's fine , "Where's your parents?"
"I'm 13 and probably at the house, I live just outside of Bubblewood."
"Oh yeah, we live there, number 2a." I said.
"Oh yeah I live like 2 minutes away." Dollie said.
"Okay shall we get you home then?" I asked.
"Please I don't want to go yet, is it okay if I come with you?" she said,
"Uh yes okay then let's go."

So we got back to our house and on the way back we found her dog! We wanted to take the dog and Dollie back to her house but she insisted she stayed. We didn't go to the cottage because we didn't want Dollie to know, well at least not yet.
"So what do you want to do?" I asked vigorously trying to

break the sound of silence that echoed in the room.
“Uh I don’t mind, we could paint our nails?” Dollie said.
"Uh okay then come upstairs then.”
“Wow, your bedroom is so big. I need a room like this.”
“Well how big is you're room?” I asked her but I'm not sure she heard everything as she had her eyes fixed to my room.
“Dollie.” I said with a little volume.
“Oh sorry I uh love your room.” she said once again.
“Shall we go outside and play frisbee or football?” I said, eagerly trying to get this strange girl out of my room.

So we played football for a little while and we all got to know her a lot better. So we invited her over again next week. We needed time to think if we should tell her about the food or not. After all not everyone could know. Plus tomorrow we had to say goodbye to beloved Milky and take him to Big Mouth.

We all, including Mum, got into Beth's car and drove only to the gate before we saw a very keen Sally Daisy trying to get over the gate.
“Sally what on earth are you doing?” Mum asked.
“Well, if it isn't Louise - changed the lock have you?”
“Seems that way.” Mum said trying not to laugh.
“Well, let me in. I've come for some of my clothes, as I'm heading to Big Mouth in a minute. .” she said acting like its normal for a woman in her 30's climbing over a gate trying to break into a little cottage.
“Uh no, I think I'll pass, plus that cottage belongs to us now. You only want to go there so you can steal the food anyway.” Tori said, “You never change.”
“Fine then I'll be on my way then, goodbye.” she said as she struggled to get down from the gate.

So she was off and so were we. She had no idea that the pass was a fake; this was going to be fun to watch.

So we drove through the gate and into the nearby garage to get our disguised bus thing to follow Sally in. We looked like a bunch of hooligans in this bus. It was full to the rim of balloons and pink fluffy stuff.

“Okay guys, we need to keep our distance, and watch her in the mirror. Try to see what she is doing. Keep your eye firmly on her.” I said.

“She's looking right at our bus!” I said in panic.

“Okay don't worry, she's probably just looking at all the balloons, did she see you?” Beth asked.

“No I don't think so.”

“Right, she took a left, we are here.”

“Right then let’s hide.” I said.

So we parked the bus in the bushes and looked through the headlights. She smugly held the pass up against the wall and obviously it didn’t work. She started shouting things like. “Oh no they tricked me! I should have seen this coming. I'm going to get them.”

It was actually really funny until she got in her car and raced away. She just said she was going to get us so we chased back to the cottage just in case.

Chapter Twenty

The big swallow...

Once we got back home, Sally was awaiting us. We just told her to go away and she did just that. I think that she was tired because she definitely wouldn't have went otherwise.
“Well that was a bit strange, normally she would bite our heads off.” Tori said, “I should know.”
“What happened when you were living with her – like was she horrible like she is now?” I asked.
“No this is the thing, she was always so lovely to me but ever since all this stuff with Big Mouth she just never has the time for me.” Tori said feeling sorry for herself.
“You was the one who said that you didn't want to see her again, I bet that she'd be just fine with you if you didn't say that.” Eve said.
“No because I said that she was still acting funny before the whole Big Mouth thing.”
“Oh please stop arguing, you’re making my head hurt.”

As we watched Sally drive off something flew out of her window. It looked like a piece of paper.
“Look something just came out of her car.” Beth said running towards it. We all ran after Beth, but suddenly she came to a stop as Sally started reversing back towards us all. Her door was open and she was screeching.
“Back off, that’s mine you nosy things.” she shouted.
We didn’t get to look at the piece of paper properly because she snatched it off us but it said something about the steel works in Far Forest closing. There's a sign saying that there is a steel works but it leads to Big Mouth so there's not actually a steel works there. It was just to put people off trying to go there.

The next day Dollie came round and asked if we wanted to go to the river with her. So we told her that we wasn't expecting her to come until next week but we still went anyway. We were free of having to think about Sally for the whole day. We all had so much fun, throwing each other into the freezing water.
"Do you live with your mum and dad?" Dollie asked.
"Yeah, well me and Eve are best friends and my mum adopted her just over a year ago. Tori lives in the cottage with Beth though because her mum is away." I tried to explain.
"Oh okay, please say yes!" Dollie said jumping up and down.
"To what? " we asked.
"Oh please can my parents come for dinner to meet yours, oh please!?" she shouted.

Well, we had agreed (not that Dollie gave us much choice) that tonight was the night we were going to meet Dollie's parents. I wasn't scared because I've had a lot of experience in meeting new people but Dollie seems to be quite full on so I can only imagine what her parents would be like.

There was a loud ringing sound that awoke me from my rather relaxing daydream. It took me a moment or two before I realised that it was indeed my phone, Dollie was phoning me.
"Hello?" I said as if I didn't know who it was.
"Hello Vesta, it's me, we're on our way." she said in reassurance.
"Okay great, I'll set the table." I said quite sarcastically.
I really didn't want to do this because I don't really know her that well. I have to give it a go I suppose.

There was an unusually loud knock on the door - of course there was only one person that could be. Dollie's loud voice was shouting greetings through the letter box.
"Hello Dollie." Mum said as she opened the door for them all to walk in.
"Hello, I'm Ally, Dollie's mum." she said.
"I'm Craig, her father. Can I make myself useful? How about the washing up."
"Uh we haven't eaten yet." my mum said.
I was right, her parents were as full on as Dollie.

So we all sat down to eat. We all had the same dinner that consisted of cauliflower cheese. This was my favourite dish and mum always loved making it and I enjoyed eating it. It was very nice and both of Dollie's parents made that crystal clear.
"Oh this is delightful, probably the very best meal ever." her mum said as she took a big gulp of 'Award winning water.'
This was certainly a very strange family, but no stranger than ours.
"Oh this is honestly so nice, how on earth can you not finish it?" Dollie said as she struggled to put the plate down after almost eating it.

"Well uh thanks for coming to dinner, we will probably see you tomorrow." I said.
"Uh actually no, sorry girls but we came to dinner today to tell you that we will be moving a long way away from here for my dad's work. We just wanted to come and say goodbye." Dollie said.

One half of me was very relieved to see the back of her, but then again one half of me for some reason didn't want to see her go.
"Oh, well I don't really know what to say."
But before any of us had the chance to break the awkward

silence, there was a very loud knock at the door.
“Uh I'll get that.” my dad said as he strolled unsurely towards the door.
I followed my dad to the door to try and get myself out of this situation, but little did I know that Sally was going to be at the door.
“Hello Mr. Marshfield.” Sally said as I backed up round the corner so that she wouldn't see me.
“I am here to see Vesta, Eve and Tori, I must ask them a question.” Sally said.
“Right well you'd better come in then.” my dad said stupidly.
I ran back into the room, whispered “excuse us”, grabbed Tori and Eve then we ran out the back door.

“Woah what are you doing? ” Tori said confusedly.
“Sally was at the door, she told my dad that she needed to ask us all a question. It has to be about that piece of paper we saw the other day.”
“Well what are we going to do?” Eve asked.
“Well...”
Before I could say anything else my phone rang. “Who is it?”
“It’s my dad.”
“Hello?”
“Hey Vesta it’s your dad. Sally's here. She wanted to ask you girls a question. Where did you lot run off to?”
“Uh, we just went for a walk.” I said.
“So, what? You just decided to leave Dollie and her parents lost for words as you just ran off?” Dad said sounding quite annoyed.
“Sorry dad.”
“Well don’t say sorry to me, it’s Dollie you need to be apologising to. Get yourselves home right now.”

We all strolled home dreading what we'd come back to. I opened the garden gate and walked towards the door as we were all trying to come up with a cover story.
“So if she does ask about the paper just say that none of us saw anything, okay?" So we were all agreed that we were going to lie to Sally's face.

“Hello Vesta, can you three come in the kitchen for a minute?” Sally asked.
“Uh yeah sure just let me apologise to Dollie first.” I said as Sally subtly dragged me back and shoved us all in the kitchen.
“What did you lot see? You know when a piece of paper fell out of my car?” she asked.
“We didn’t see anything, nothing at all.” Eve said looking terrified.
“Don’t lie to me girls, I know you did because you picked it up and looked at it.” she said as we all looked at each other, hoping that one of the others would say something.
“Oh that, yes we did see something.” Eve said.
“Ah yes we did.” Tori added.
And now it was obviously down to me to finish it off.
“We just saw a part that said ‘Carl's Cleaning’”. I said desperately trying to recall the advert that was next to the title.

“Do you need a cleaner?” Eve asked, “My dad’s very good at that sort of stuff isn't he Vesta?”
“Oh yes, he loves cleaning.” I said trying to sound enthusiastic.
“Good, good, well if I ever need a cleaner I'll ask your dad. Come on I'm leaving now.” she said so fast we could hardly make it out.
We walked back into the room where Dollie and her parents were, trying to figure out how Sally believed us.

"Sorry Dollie, uh I needed a walk after we heard you were leaving." I said.
"Oh that's alright. Well, we'd better be off. Goodbye girls, it's been lovely hanging out with you all." she said.
"Well it's been interesting but really fun." I said smiling at her as she walked out the door wishing us the best.

"We can't leave it like that." Tori said.
"What do you mean?"
"Well, we need to give her a leaving present or something."
"Yeah you're right, I've got it." Eve shouted, "Listen, we took lots of photos together yeah? So I'll go down to the library now to print then out. You two go to the shop and buy a scrap book, them meet me outside the toilets, Go."
So we followed Eve's orders and headed to town.
"Do you like Eve's idea?" I asked Tori.
"Yeah it's such a good idea, we could write little messages under the photos too, it's going to be so fun, I love scrap books."

Once we got to the shop we started scanning the shelves for a decent scrap book. Even though we've only known Dollie for a little while, we still felt like it was a good idea to do this for her.
"Ooh look here's a good one." Tori said pointing to a pink and yellow book.
"Yeah that looks good, do you have any arts and craft things at the cottage?"
"No I left all that at my grandad's house. Don't you have anything?" Tori asked.
"Well that's it, I don't have a lot so should we buy a new batch?"
"Yeah how much money do you have?" she asked.
"I've got like £10 I think."
"Okay that should be enough."

We bought everything and strolled off to meet Eve at the toilets. She was already there with loads of paper in her arms.
“Got it?” she asked.
“Yeah, we bought lots of art and craft stuff too.” I said.
“Good, look at all these. Let’s look at them properly over some fish and chips.” Eve suggested.
So after Eve bought us fish and chips we headed back home.

“Would you care to explain what happened earlier?” Dad said as we walked in the door.
“Sorry dad, we weren't expecting Dollie to tell us that, I just panicked and ran.”
“Well that’s alright I suppose, go upstairs for a bit, I need to do some cleaning.” he said as we ran up the stairs giggling.

We threw everything on the floor and started cutting and sticking.
“Vesta, you're good at writing poems and all that stuff so you do some messages.” Eve ordered.
We stayed in my room for a good two hours before we finally decided that it was time to stop and go for a walk.
“Ah that was a very productive two hours, let’s go and paddle in the waterfall.” Eve suggested.
“Can you paddle in a waterfall?” I asked.
“The river in front of it, you know what I mean.” she argued.

“So when is Dollie leaving?” Eve asked.
“I'm not too sure, I don’t think she said. But we could go to her house and drop it off.” I suggested.
“Yeah that’s a great idea. Wait, does any of you know where she lives because I don’t.” Tori said.
“Well, when we met her she said that she lives just the other side of Bubble wood, remember?”

“Oh yeah, but the other side of Bubble wood is Far Forest. You don’t think she lives there do you?” Eve asked.
“Well she must do, Far Forest is a very small place and it’s all surrounding the steel works or as we know it, Big Mouth.” Tori said in utter shock.
“Right then well we'd better be getting back home. We'll go now, get the book and go.” Eve suggested.

So we had a lovely walk back. Brushing our damp feet on the silky grass.
“Okay, Vesta you go in and get the book, while me and Tori get the bikes.” Eve ordered.
We rode all the way to Far Forest, soaring through the wind like a bird.
“How exactly are we going to figure out which house it is?” Tori said, looking around.
“No... Sally, its Sally.” I said in utter shock.
“Sally? What are you doing here?” Eve asked.

“Girls, oh hello girls. What are you doing here?” she asked, trying to cover the fact that she'd just been caught.
“We came to find Dollie, your turn.”
“Oh I just came for a walk.”
“Oh no you're not getting out of it that easily.” Tori said, definitely enjoying shouting at Sally.
“Fine, if I can't have Big Mouth then no one can!” she shouted as she ran in the gate that leads to Big Mouth.
“Stop her!” I shouted as we all charged towards the squealing woman.
“That’s what the poster meant when it said Far Forest Steel Works closing.” Eve said.

Eventually, we caught up with her and questioned her. She basically said what we already knew, how she was planning to close Big Mouth. The worst thing about all of this is that we have no say in the matter because Sally owns

Big Mouth. We needed to reason with her but, try as we might, she was determined to sell up to her long-lost cousin over in Australia.

“Sally, Big Mouth is our life.” Eve said desperately trying to get Sally to listen.
“No, I'm sorry but my cousin is offering far too much money,” she said as she ran off cackling.

We all slowly walked around Far Forest in disbelief that Big Mouth was going.
“Look, there's Dollie.” I shouted as we all started calling her.
“Dollie, come here.”
“Oh hi guys.” she said in shock.
“Uh what are you doing here?”
“We came to give you this before you left.” I said, handing her the scrap book.
“Oh wow I love it, it’s amazing.” she said, flicking through the pages, “What's the matter with you lot?” she asked, looking confused.
“Oh nothing, we’re just upset you’re leaving.” Tori said, trying to come up with something that didn’t sound completely ridiculous

We all said our goodbyes to Dollie and her parents, before heading back home. We felt that we had to break the news to Mum, so we got her a cup of lemon tea and told her. Obviously she was devastated, but as she pointed out, we don’t know the next batch of food so we won’t get attached. However, the food all leave for Big Mouth one last time tomorrow, so we decided to pay one last visit to the cottage.

We knocked very loudly on the door.
"Hello?" came a voice that sounded very much like Beth's.
"Hey, it's us." Eve shouted.
"Oh hi, yes come in." she shouted through the old wooden door.
"Hey, we just wanted to spend some time with the foods before they go." I explained.

So we went in and played lots of games with the foods, we also read them stories. We obviously had to explain the sad news to Beth as well.
"What? But I can't walk away now." Beth said, beginning to look like she was about to cry.
"Don't worry Beth, maybe it's time to move on now anyway." I said, trying to process what actually just came out my mouth.

In the end Beth understood that she had to move on, just like the rest of us. It was time to say goodbye to Big Mouth for good. Before we left, we gave all the food massive cuddles and told them never to be afraid. After that emotional day it was time to go home and sleep.

Beth rang the next day and said that she was thinking about moving away from Bubblewood.
"What? But why?" I asked.
"Well there's just far too many memories. If I stay here I will just miss the foods, not to mention the house, it's just best to move on, like you said."
"Well we didn't mean to leave Bubblewood. Where will you go?" Eve asked.
"Well one of my old friends from the witchcraft school I used to go to said that she has opened up a shop in Scotland. She said that I could work and live there with

her." she said rather teary.
Then she hung up.

"We have to go find her and say a proper goodbye." I said.
So we ran down to the cottage to find her.
"Beth please stop." we said as she started the engine of the rather old-looking car.
"What do you mean by a proper goodbye?" she asked as she stumbled out of her rusty car.
"We need to say goodbye and mostly thank you for everything you have done for us." I pleaded.
"Oh alright then if you insist." she said as we all walked into the cottage.
"Okay so first of all, what's going to happen to Tori?"
"Well she can live with you can't she? Or she could go back to her grandad's." Beth said, clearly not knowing the circumstances.
"Sally is living with her grandad, remember?" I argued.
"Oh yes well I'm sorry girls but I'm going now."

Well that was that then. We spent the rest of the day sorting out Tori's living arrangements. We all finally decided that Tori could stay in the attic for a while. After another exhausting day, we all went to sleep surprisingly very early.

The next morning, as we all took a stroll through the woods to ease off the drama, we saw Dollie and her parents driving off with two removal vans behind them. We waved them off, but I had a feeling that this wasn't going to be the last we saw of Dollie..

Chapter Eleven

The inside...

“Wow, what on earth? What is this? No it can’t be. Stop. Wait. So it’s true then, you really can talk to foods?” said Eve.
“What do you mean ‘so it’s true?’ Who's told you?” she said.
“Oh no one honest, me and Eve read your file. We know you used to be a student at our school." I said.
“Yeah that’s true, they didn't believe me. I saw the food first when I was 11. A milk carton said ‘Don’t pick me, I have a hole on my tongue.’ Honestly, I didn’t think it was real either until day after day they kept on talking. Then Mr. Cream came along, he was my history teacher. At first he didn't believe me, but then they started talking to him. The horrid headteacher at the time, Mr. Bran, he sent us both off to the same asylum and the same room!” Sally said.
“But why are you here?” I said.
“Well dear, we raise the food here until they’re two years old.”
“What happens then?” I said.
“They go to a place called Big Mouth. It’s a beautiful place.” she said.

“Oh and by the way girls, I have someone I want you two to meet.” she said, sounding as if an amazing thing was behind this mysterious door.
When she opened the door a young girl with big eyes and rosy checks popped out.
“Girls I would like to introduce you to my daughter, Tori.”
“Uh hey Tori my name is Eve and this is my best friend Vesta.”

“Alright guys how are you?” Tori asked.
“Uh yeah we're fine. So did you know about your mother’s food?” I asked.
“Yeah, but only since the other day.” she said.
So after Miss Daisy filled us in about her food we went over to Tori's house for tea, we all became really good friends.

Over the course of the next few weeks, we all got to know the food better.
“Hello Shake, aren't you growing." I said.
"Yeah I don't want to leave you.” he said,
“The really sad thing is that once they are all two years old, they have to go to a place called Big Mouth. If they go a day later then they will be trapped in the house forever.”

We didn't want to tell Kristie because she would tell everyone in sight, so we told, and showed them all, to Oscar.
“Right Oscar, I don't want you to be surprised or nervous, but there are a few things I want to introduce you to.” I said.
“Oh should I be scared? I'm going to tell Kristie.” he said sounding so childish.
We told him not to tell anyone.
“This is Mr. Hot.” I said.
“Oh well I wasn’t expecting that. Er hello, uh my name is Oscar, I'm their brother.” he said.
I must say I was expecting him to freak out a little more.

“So you're not scared of them?” I asked.
“No Vest, to be honest I already knew about them. So does mum, Sally was in school with her. Mind you, we both were told that they got extinct.” he said.
“What? You both knew how...why...what?” I said with so much confusion, I was so unaware of any of this.

Printed in Poland
by Amazon Fulfillment
Poland Sp. z o.o., Wrocław

52606051R00042